FRED
IN CHARGE

The Adventures of Fred
Published by Fawcett Columbine

FRED TO THE RESCUE
FRED IN CHARGE
FRED AND THE PET SHOW PANIC
FRED SAVES THE DAY

FRED
IN CHARGE

by Leslie McGuire

Illustrated by Dave Henderson

Fawcett Columbine • New York

CONTENTS

Chapter Ten: An Indian Would Be
Better   65

CHAPTER ONE

RELIEF IS SPELLED "W-I-N-T-E-R"

A lot of folks do not like winter. I love winter. I know it's freezing. The ground is covered with ice and snow. You can't go outside much. It gets dark too early. Well, those are the things I love about winter. Winter is my best time of year.

I also love winter because I am very furry. Maybe I should explain. You see, I am Fred. I am the Duff family dog. I am a Saint Bernard. Saint Bernards are those dogs that save people. They carry little barrels of brandy under their chins. They are supposed to give the brandy to the people they save. I think brandy is a stupid thing to give people. Chicken soup would be much better. But no

1

one asks me these things. They should. I know a lot about what is good for people.

Anyway, the Duffs live in a little town named Big Bluff. It is called Big Bluff because the town has a big cliff that goes right down to the harbor. The Duffs live right on top of the big bluff. They like to call it Duff's Bluff.

I hate the bluff. Someone is always getting too close to the edge. Then I have to rescue them. Usually I have to rescue Mr. Duff when he mows the lawn. He thinks he has to mow the lawn every weekend. Every weekend I have to save him. Every weekend he calls me a fathead.

Mrs. Duff doesn't need much rescuing. For that, I am very grateful. Katie Duff is a teenager. She doesn't need rescuing. What she needs is watching. She's very bad at crossing streets. But I just throw myself in front of her whenever she tries to cross against the light. She doesn't like it. But safe is safe, I always say. Arnie Duff, on the other hand, is a big problem. Not that he's big.

He's little. I'm taller than Arnie is when Arnie is standing up and I am sitting down.

The trouble with Arnie is his new glasses. Before last summer, he couldn't see anything at all. Now he has glasses, and he can see everything. This does not help. He is always rushing off to get a better look at something ridiculous like a bug or a sports car. Arnie never looks where he's going. I spend most of my time rescuing Arnie.

That's why I love winter. There's hardly any rescuing to do. It is cold, so no grass grows. That means no lawn mowing near the bluff. That means I don't have to rescue Mr. Duff.

Also, during the winter, the kids don't spend all day at the playground. That means I don't have to spend all day saving Arnie from the slide or the swings.

There are no picnics, no cookouts, and no camping trips. Phew! The best part is that the kids are in school for most of the day. I can lie around in a heap.

There is only one small problem with winter. That is Arnie's birthday. Not that Arnie shouldn't have a birthday. It's just the birthday party I object to. The party is always a disaster. Hundreds of kids come. Well, maybe not hundreds. But it *feels* like hundreds.

At the birthday party there are noisemakers, and party hats, and awful games. The only good part about the party is the kids spill food all over the house. They also forget to watch their pieces of cake. I eat everything they spill. I also eat all unguarded pieces of cake.

I'm not being mean when I eat their food. I do it for their own good. Kids shouldn't eat food that falls on the floor, right? It's dirty. They might get sick. They also shouldn't have too much sugar. Sugar is bad for their teeth, right? I eat all that stuff to be helpful. I am a very thoughtful dog.

I must admit I enjoy the food. I feel it is a very small reward for all the trouble I go through on Arnie's birthday.

Well, this year, Arnie's birthday celebra-

tion began too soon. I was lying around on the living room rug. I was enjoying the peace. I was trying to keep calm about Arnie's birthday. Then the phone rang. Katie answered it. I didn't pay any attention. Katie is always talking on the phone.

Then Mrs. Duff got on the phone. Then Arnie got on, too. Everyone was saying things like "Neat!" and "Great!" and "How wonderful!" and "This is going to be so much fun!"

I had a bad feeling. Anything the Duffs think is fun or great or neat usually ends up meaning more work for me.

Was I ever right! Grandma Duff was coming to visit. She was coming just for Arnie's tenth birthday party! Oh no! A double disaster!

CHAPTER TWO

GET ME TO THE TRAIN ON TIME

The news about Grandma Duff did not make me happy. I went outside to talk to Winston. Winston is the dog who lives next door. Winston's face looks like he crashed into a wall. But that is because he is a pug. Pugs are supposed to look like that. Because of his short, rumpled nose, Winston makes weird noises. For example, he sounds like a clogged drain when he laughs.

"Grandma Duff is coming today," I groaned. "She'll be here for a week! Maybe I should leave town."

"What's so bad about Grandma Duff?" Winston asked.

"She's little," I said. "She's weak. She's

7

old. She can probably hardly climb the stairs."

"So what," said Winston. "How much trouble can she get into?"

"Are you crazy?" I said. "Look at that sheet of ice on the sidewalk!"

"So what," said Winston. He sounded like a broken record.

"She will probably slip and break every bone in her body!" I snapped. "And I, Fred, am responsible for her safety and well-being!"

Just then, something with four hard points landed on my back. It screeched. I jumped.

It was Fudge.

Fudge is a kitten. He came to live with the Duffs on Halloween night. That was the worst night of my life—so far. It was mostly because of Fudge.

The kids found Fudge in the old Griswold mansion. But that is another story. Fudge is black and white. They named him Vanilla Fudge, which is a sickeningly cute name.

They call him Fudge for short. I do not think he's cute.

Until recently, Fudge wasn't too bad. Except that he insists on calling me "Mom." I hate that. But Fudge discovered Sam and Janet. Sam and Janet are the two cats who belong to the next-door neighbors, the Evenings. Sam and Janet have been giving Fudge cat lessons. They said they were afraid Fudge would grow up thinking he was a dog.

Personally, I think that would have been best. Dogs are brave. Dogs are loyal. Dogs are helpful. Cats just sit around and wash.

That is, unless they're making trouble.

Sam and Janet were giving Fudge his pouncing lesson. Fudge was pouncing on me. I hate that, too. I shook Fudge off my back and growled at him.

"How was that pounce, Mom?" Fudge said with a cat smile.

I growled even harder. He tried to lick my nose, but he missed.

Just then, Mrs. Duff called me into the house. Fudge came right in behind me.

Maybe they were planning to yell at Fudge for pouncing on me, I thought. Or, better yet, give me a little snack. I was wrong. Everyone had their coats on.

"You stay here," said Arnie. "We're going to pick up Grandma at the train station."

They all rushed out the door. It slammed behind them. Then I heard it lock.

I love the Duffs very much. But sometimes they have no sense. They were going to the train station without me! Anyone who knows anything knows that train stations are very, very dangerous places! I had to get to that train station!

I checked every door and window in the house. They were all locked. This was a problem. But it was not a big one. They do not call me the Great Houdini of Dogs for nothing. I can get out of anything, just like the great escape artist, Harry Houdini. He could get out of a locked cage, while he was handcuffed and blindfolded. I am even better.

I was heading to the basement when I saw something dreadful. Fudge was shredding the latest copy of *Natural History* magazine.

"What do you think you're doing?" I howled.

"Shredding practice," said Fudge.

"Is that part of your cat lessons?" I asked. "Because if it is, you can stop right this second!"

"But . . ." Fudge started to say.

"No buts," I said. "I happen to be in the middle of a very good article about South American cockroaches."

When I'm nervous, I eat magazines. Lately I've been nervous. But when I eat, I like to read. I have learned quite a few helpful and amazing things.

"Can you teach me how to read, Mom?" Fudge asked.

"Only if you stop shredding that article this instant!" I said.

Right away I was sorry I said that. I did not want to have anything to do with Fudge.

But on the other hand, knowledge is far

12

more important than shredding and pouncing. I couldn't make up my mind. Teaching Fudge could mean trouble. The only thing worse than a dumb cat is a smart cat.

"Oh, thank you, Mom," said Fudge, giving me a sappy look. He pointed his paw to a big word in an advertisement for Hawaiian cruises. "What does this mean?"

"I can't start reading lessons today," I said. I backed out of the room. "I have an important meeting to go to."

I raced down to the basement. I hoped that by tomorrow, Fudge would forget the whole thing.

I was in luck. There was a little tiny window. It wasn't locked. It was the old coal chute. There was a handy pile of coal and boxes right under it.

I climbed the boxes. A few fell down. There was a crunching noise. I shoved against the window with my nose. It opened. I was on my way!

Of course.

CHAPTER THREE

MORE WORK FOR FRED

I ran down to Main Street. Then I turned right onto Railroad Avenue. I could hear the train whistle in the distance. I knew I would make it.

I got to the platform just in time. Of course, the Duffs were all standing too close to the edge of the tracks. At any second, a giant train would be roaring into the station. It would be going at least 190 miles an hour. But did they think about that? No.

I threw myself at Katie because she was the closest. I knocked her back to a safe place near the station house. It was a good move. The rest of the Duffs came rushing over to help her up. Arnie grabbed my collar.

"Be careful, Fred," he said. "Don't get in the way of the train!"

Silly boy. He thought he was keeping me safe. You see how clever I am? Do you see how silly they can be? I got the whole family away from a speeding train. And they thought they were keeping *me* away from the speeding train.

Katie was not happy. She screamed and yelled at me for a while. She said something about getting her all covered with black stuff. Katie started hitting her pants, and big puffs of coal dust flew in the air. Mrs. Duff looked puzzled. But before she could say anything, the train pulled in. It screeched to a stop. They forgot all about Katie and the coal dust, and started looking for Grandma Duff.

Well, about five thousand people got off the train. I was hoping Grandma Duff had forgotten to come. But no such luck. Soon a little old lady wearing a big, hairy coat and a woolly knit hat got off the train. She was carrying two huge suitcases. She didn't look

16

too weak. But I would keep my eye on her anyway.

After everybody hugged and kissed, we got in the car to go home. That is, the Duffs got in the car. They made me walk home. Katie said I was too dirty. I can't understand why some people can get so upset about a little coal dust.

But I didn't mind. It was crowded in the car. Even without me. Two big Duffs, one medium-sized Duff, one small Duff, one Grandma Duff, and two big suitcases is a lot for a car.

After Grandma Duff got settled into the guest room, we all sat around. Things seemed pretty calm. Except for Fudge. He had to sit in Grandma Duff's lap. That would have been fine, but Grandma Duff was knitting. I guess grandmothers are always knitting. Anyway, Fudge had to play with the wool.

Fudge rolled it. He pushed it. He chased

it. He wound the wool all over the place. He tied the couch to the chair, to the lamp, to the coffee table, to my tail.

Everyone thought it was cute. I didn't.

It was dangerous. If someone got up, they could trip on the wool. They might break a leg. They could crack their heads open on the floor.

"Cut that out!" I said. Maybe it came out like a growl.

Fudge looked very sad.

"I'm sorry, Mom," he said.

"Don't call me Mom!"

"I'll never do it again, Mom," he said.

And that's when he kissed me. I didn't back up fast enough. It was gross. I hate being kissed by that cat. Especially when people are watching. But Fudge is a born troublemaker. I know he does it on purpose, just to make me mad. I checked the windows to make sure Winston hadn't seen it. Or worse, Sam and Janet. Of course, it was pitch-dark outside. I couldn't see a thing.

"Isn't that sweet," said Grandma Duff.

"Look how well those two get along. It's unusual."

You bet it is unusual. The truth is, I once made an insane promise. It was by accident. It was right before Fudge came to live with us.

I promised never to chase another cat as long as I lived. This is the only mistake I have ever made. I should have promised not to chase cats for a month or two. Oh well. It was a bad night. But that is another story.

Of course, Fudge kept right on playing with the ball of wool. Finally Arnie got up and untied everything. Everyone thought the whole thing was very cute and sweet.

Fudge finally fell asleep on Grandma Duff's lap. Soon they were all yawning.

When everyone was tucked safely in bed, I went out. The one good thing about nighttime is that everyone is asleep. They can't get into much trouble when they're asleep. That is good for me. I have less to worry about.

Winston was outside.

"How'd it go?" he asked.

"Things could have been worse," I said.

I was about to say it was a nice night when a wet thing landed on my nose. It was a snowflake. Then another wet thing landed on my eye. I looked up. A flurry of snowflakes was coming at me. It looked as if a feather pillow had just been ripped open.

"Oh, no," I groaned. "Things could have been worse. By tomorrow, they will definitely be worse!"

CHAPTER FOUR

TRIPLE DISASTER

It snowed very hard that night. By the next morning, everything was covered with snow. The sheet of ice on the sidewalk was under a foot of snow.

Fudge and I went outside early in the morning. Of course, as soon as Fudge stepped outside, he disappeared. Fudge had never seen snow before. He jumped off the top step of the porch and went *phumph*. Gone. Only the tip of his tail showed. I had to rescue him. He was very grateful. Fudge stayed on the porch after that. I went inside the house to check on the rest of the family.

Mr. Duff woke up early. He groaned when he looked out the window. I should tell you that Mr. Duff is very big. He is bald. He wears glasses, just like Arnie. When he went outside, he was bundled up in so much stuff that he looked like a big mountain of clothes.

While Mr. Duff was shoveling snow, Mrs. Duff and Grandma Duff were in the kitchen making a big roast. Arnie and Katie hung around slicing apples for pie and peeling sweet potatoes. I hung around hoping for a few nice scraps.

One of the things I love about Mrs. Duff is that she is very forgetful. She forgets to put food away. This is good for me. Leaving food out for too long is unhealthy. It could go bad. It might make people sick. That is why I eat it all up. I also like to taste things before anyone else sits down to eat. After all, what if something isn't right? If I try it first and get sick, then they'll know not to eat it, correct? Correct. Of course, I do this just to protect my family. I am a very noble dog.

But there were too many people in the

kitchen. No one gave me a chance to taste things.

Soon Mr. Duff came inside. The walks were only half-cleared. But he said he needed a rest. His face was as red as a beet. It was pretty cold out there. Mr. Duff picked up the newspaper and went right up to bed. Since nothing was happening in the kitchen, I went along. I figured I could get some quiet reading in.

I read a very interesting article about what to do when the pipes freeze. Well, it wasn't *that* interesting. But you never know when it will come in handy. After about an hour, Mr. Duff started sneezing. His nose started running. His eyes started watering. He was coughing and wheezing like an old car. He sounded a lot like Winston, actually.

Grandma Duff came right upstairs. She brought him some tea. She wrapped him up in three sweaters and a quilt. I was afraid he would smother under all that stuff. People would be a lot better off if they had fur like dogs.

After that, Grandma Duff started running up and down the stairs to check on Mr. Duff. That meant I had to run up and down the stairs after her. After all, she was little. She was old. She was weak. She might fall. I had to keep my eye on her.

During Grandma's fifth trip upstairs, I heard a scream and a crash from the kitchen. Grandma Duff and I raced down to see what was wrong.

Well, it was good news and bad news. The good news was that the roast was on the floor. Mrs. Duff had dropped the pan taking it out of the oven. The bad news was that the reason Mrs. Duff dropped the pan was that she sprained her back.

Mrs. Duff was holding on to the kitchen table. She said she couldn't move.

Unfortunately, I wasn't able to get at the roast. Grandma Duff told Katie and Arnie to clean up while she took care of Mrs. Duff.

Grandma Duff held on to Mrs. Duff. She helped Mrs. Duff upstairs and into bed. She

25

put pillows under Mrs. Duff's knees, and called the doctor.

I don't know how Grandma Duff did any of it. Mrs. Duff is big, and Grandma Duff is little. Maybe Grandma Duff *is* strong. There is no other explanation.

Anyway, the doctor said that Mrs. Duff had to stay in bed and not move a muscle. Grandma Duff said she would take care of everything.

What a mess. The Duffs' bedroom looked like a hospital. Mr. and Mrs. Duff were both in bed. They were both sick. Grandma Duff was in charge of everything. And I was in charge of her.

She ran up and down the stairs all day. So did I. We must have gone up and down the stairs a hundred times. By dinnertime, I was exhausted. Grandma Duff was still going strong!

I fell asleep at nine o'clock that night. By morning, everything would be back to normal, I thought. But by morning, things were worse.

It snowed again all night.

Grandma Duff was down in the kitchen at six-thirty making breakfast. When she saw the snow, she smiled and patted me on the head.

"What fun!" she said when Katie and Arnie came down. "Today is Arnie's birthday! We can have a snow party! But first, we'll go out and shovel the front walk!"

Katie groaned, but Arnie didn't. He said, "Neato! Beth and Mike can come early to help!"

Beth Woods and Mike Peese are Arnie's best friends. Beth's father is a scientist. He collects things like spiders and snakes and frogs. So does Beth. She says she's rescuing them. From what, I ask? Spiders, snakes, and frogs don't need rescuing. They are fine right where they are—wherever that is. But at least her heart is in the right place.

Mike likes to take pictures of things. He is always carrying a camera. This is good, because he gets great pictures of me rescuing the Duffs. For some reason, the Duffs don't like the pictures. Especially Katie Duff. I guess teenagers are funny about things like that. She'll get over it.

Anyway, an hour later, everyone was outside shoveling the front walk. It was cold. It was wet. I was still tired from following Grandma Duff up and down stairs. I could hardly stand up. And my day had just started. A truckload of wild kids was about to enter my happy home.

Three disasters in twenty-four hours is more than any dog can stand—even me, Fred.

CHAPTER FIVE

PIN-THE-TAIL-ON-THE-FAMILY-DOG

After we shoveled the front walk, we had to get ready for the party. I still don't understand birthdays. I understand why kids get presents. But I don't understand why they have to have all those children come over.

Actually, that is not true. I am beginning to see that the only reason kids have birthday parties is to get presents. If you invite two kids to a party, you get two presents. If you invite fifty kids, you get fifty presents. All those presents are good for the birthday boy. But they're not good for the family dog.

The party was supposed to begin at twelve o'clock. It was now nine-thirty. Only two and one-half hours until the dreaded invasion! Grandma Duff spent the morning running up and down the stairs taking care of Mr. and Mrs. Duff. While she was doing that, Arnie and Katie were in the kitchen. They were baking a cake. Grandma Duff was helping—in between trips.

By the time Arnie and Katie put the cake in the oven, the kitchen was a mess. There was flour and sugar and icing all over the place. It was just as well that Mrs. Duff couldn't get out of bed. She would have gotten *really* sick if she had seen that mess. Unhappily, none of it was edible. Otherwise I would have done my part to clean up.

After that, Arnie and Katie made party hats and party favors. They set the table with a paper tablecloth, paper plates, and paper cups. They blew up balloons, which Fudge popped. They put noisemakers on the table. Ugh. Party noisemakers are a dog's nightmare. They make a very, very loud sound. It really hurts our delicate ears. They even put a party hat on me.

I took the party hat off. It wasn't too difficult. But the rubber band pulled out about thirty of my hairs. After that, Arnie and Katie put up a game. It was a terrible game. Pin-the-Tail-on-the-Donkey.

At twelve o'clock the doorbell rang. Enter the maniacs! A hundred kids came bouncing into the living room. Well, maybe it was only ten. Things went fine—at first. While Arnie opened his presents, the kids sat sort of still.

Right after that, they ate cake and ice cream. I got a few pieces of cake. It was actually pretty good. I was surprised. The cake hadn't looked too good while Katie and Arnie were making it.

While everyone ate, there wasn't too much running around. But then it was game time. That is when things got completely out of hand.

Pin-the-Tail-on-the-Donkey is a game that should be banned. The first thing they do is hang a big picture of a donkey on the wall. The donkey has no tail. Then all the kids stand in line. Each kid gets a turn. But first they put a blindfold on the kid. Then they hand the kid a paper tail with a tack in it. Then—and this is the crazy part—they spin the kid around three times . . . just to get him confused. After that, the kid goes staggering around the room looking for the back end of the donkey. The kid who gets his tail pinned the closest to the end of the donkey wins a prize.

Well, I don't have to tell you how dangerous *that* was.

Beth pinned the tail on the lampshade. Willie pinned the tail on the couch. John pinned the tail on the bathroom door. Jenny pinned the tail on the window. There were tails pinned everyplace but on the donkey. Forget about the back end. They weren't even close.

Not one of those children was smart enough to peek. If it were *me* wearing that blindfold, I would have tilted my head up. I could at least have figured out where I was going. But did any of them do that? Nope. Not even one. Where had they been all their lives? Under a rock?

When it was Arnie's turn, I decided to give him a little help. After all, Arnie was the birthday boy. I thought he deserved the prize.

They blindfolded him. They spun him around three times. Off he went. He was headed straight for the messy table. I walked over and gave him a little push. I was planning to head him in the direction of the donkey. It was a great plan. But Arnie isn't easy to move. Especially when he gets it into his little head to go someplace.

Well, they should have called that game Pin-the-Tail-on-the-Family-Dog, instead. Because that is what happened. Arnie tripped over me. He pinned the donkey tail on my ear. OUCH!

Poor Arnie yelled louder than I did. It was terrible. But I am a very brave dog. Grandma Duff came running. So did Beth and Mike and Katie.

Even though I was fine, they insisted on putting a bandage on my ear. I wasn't even bleeding! The funny part was that Fudge was more upset than anyone. He kept following me around, trying to lick my ear.

"Get lost, Fudge," I kept saying.

"I'm kissing the boo-boo," Fudge kept saying. "That will make it better."

"The thing that will make it better is if you leave me alone," I kept saying.

Fudge didn't seem to hear a word. Sometimes I wonder if he is deaf.

Anyway, Willie won the prize. He was the one who pinned the tail on the couch. The couch was the closest to the back end of the donkey. I should have won the prize. But it was a silly prize. What would I have done with a little plastic car?

That's when Grandma Duff said, "I have a great idea! Let's go play games in the snow!"

Aaargh! I was still a mess from the games in the house!

CHAPTER SIX

WINTER WONDERLAND MY FOOT!

"Look!" said Grandma Duff when we got outside. "A winter wonderland!"

I didn't think it was so wonderful. Everyone was having fun but me. Even Fudge was having fun. I had work to do.

It had snowed more during the party. That meant there was snow on the walks again. Grandma Duff decided to shovel the walks again. What was the point? It was still snowing. They would need more shoveling in an hour! But whatever Grandma wants, Grandma gets. I had to stick very close to her just in case she fell.

Katie had invited her clumsy boyfriend, Pete, over. Pete is nice, but he doesn't seem to know where all his arms and legs are going. He was shoveling the walks, too. Pete fell down a hundred times. But at least he stayed away from the bluff.

Getting too close to the bluff was the real problem. It was all Grandma Duff's fault. She told all those little kids to make snowmen. She said it would clear a lot of the snow off the grass. What is wrong with snow on the grass? Why not just let it melt?

Anyway, they rolled giant balls of snow all over the front yard. Then they rolled giant balls of snow all over the backyard. Of course, they got too close to the edge of the bluff. I had to race back and forth between the kids and Grandma Duff. I had to watch the kids in case they got too close to the bluff. I had to watch Grandma Duff in case she fell.

Anyone who knows anything knows that you cannot be in two places at one time.

On top of it all, that silly Fudge decided to work on pouncing practice. He was ambushing me every three minutes. He jumped on me from bushes, trees, porch railings, and swing sets. My nerves were shot.

Winston, of course, thought the whole thing was funny.

"It's a good thing," said Winston. "Once Fudge knows how to attack, you won't ever have to rescue him."

"Who would attack Fudge?" I asked. "I don't have to rescue him from attackers. I have to rescue him from himself!"

"Practice makes perfect!" said Winston.

"Blow it out your nose," I said. "Let him practice on you!"

Winston made his clogged drain noise. I was not amused.

I got to the backyard just in time to see Katie rolling a ball of snow right over to the edge of the bluff. I raced over and shoved her back into the hedge. It was a brilliant rescue. Happily, Mike had his camera ready. He took the picture. It was one of my better rescues. I decided to get that picture as soon as it was developed. I would drop it off at the local newspaper office. I was sure this time they would put it on the front page.

As I was daydreaming about the headline . . . "DOG SAVES GIRL FROM DEATH" . . . I took my eyes off Katie.

Next thing I knew, Mike was howling. Katie was trying to get the camera away from him. She was threatening to destroy the film, destroy his camera, and then destroy Mike.

I couldn't understand her problem. So she had her hat over one eye, and a lot of snow in her face. So what! So she was lying on her back with her feet up in the air. So what!

I stepped in to save Mike. I risked serious injury from Katie. She was very grouchy. But I have read that teenagers are moody and hard to handle. I could have told you that! She finally gave up and stomped into the house. Good. One less person to keep my eye on.

Then Grandma Duff had another great idea. She taught the kids how to make snow angels. Soon all five hundred kids were lying

around in the snow flapping their arms and legs. Well, maybe there were only ten kids. But they were getting caught in snow drifts. They were rolling around. They weren't watching what they were doing! They were being silly and giggly. It was very danger-ous!

While I was forced to run around like a chicken, Fudge was still pouncing on me. I could hear Winston sniggering next door. Sam and Janet were watching from a tree branch near the house. I was about to tell them all to get lost. Then I saw Arnie flap-ping out of the corner of my eye. He was try-ing to get up by rolling. He was rolling right toward the cliff!

The real problem was Arnie's snowsuit. Let me explain about snowsuits. They are big, one-piece things that cover children from the tops of their heads to the bottoms of their feet. They are made out of some fat material that won't bend. Once a kid is inside a snowsuit, his arms and legs stick out. He can't bend anything. Once a kid falls down wearing a snowsuit, he can't get up again.

There was only one solution. I had to drag Arnie over to the porch. That way, Arnie could hang on to the railing and pull himself up.

I grabbed Arnie by one boot and started pulling. The boot was the only part of Arnie that would fit in my mouth. The rest of Arnie was too fat with snowsuit, sweaters, scarves, hats, and who knows what.

But Arnie was not helping me. He flapped and yanked and squirmed. By the time I got him over to the porch, his boot came off.

Arnie called me a fathead! All the kids laughed!

I carefully put the boot on his chest. I sat on the porch swing. My feelings were very hurt. I don't mind when Mr. Duff or Katie calls me a fathead. But I do mind when Arnie does it. He has never done that before!

Arnie was mad, but of course, he calmed down when he saw how upset I was. He came over and gave me a big hug. That made me feel better. But only a bit.

I was so tired from chasing after Grandma Duff and the kids all day, I thought I would never be able to move again. But my troubles were just beginning.

CHAPTER SEVEN

NO REST FOR THE DOG

Well, I figured that by this time, all the little maniacs would be tired. But they weren't. Then Grandma Duff had a perfectly awful idea for what to do next.

She told them to build a snow fort!

Here is how it is done. But I don't suggest that anyone try it. Even with an adult and a dog watching you, it is far too unsafe.

Here is my advice. Avoid this snow activity as if it were spinach—even if you like spinach.

"Building a snow fort is easy," said Grandma Duff.

Did she learn this from an Eskimo? I would have asked her, but she was too busy smacking blobs of snow into a big square block.

All the kids joined in. Soon Beth and Mike came over. They made big blocks of snow, too. The blocks were sort of like big bricks. Willie and Jennie and John made blocks, too. Soon they had lots of blocks. They stacked a row of blocks in a circle. Then they sprayed it with the hose. The water makes the blocks freeze solid. It also makes them stick together.

Next they piled on another row of blocks. This went on for hours.

I had to rush all over trying to keep an eye on them. At first they were using snow that was close to the house. But then they needed too many blocks. They all went off in different directions. Some got too close to the cliff. Some got too close to the street. Some actually went next door!

It was the same problem I'd had before. But this time there was a big difference. Earlier in the day I had more energy. Now I was exhausted!

But things were getting worse. As the fort got higher and higher, it became more dangerous. I knew the whole fort would fall down any minute. And once it fell, it would squish anyone who was standing nearby.

Building that snow fort was an insane plan. But what could I do? Whatever Grandma Duff wanted, Grandma Duff got. The kids kept right on building the fort.

I tried to tell Grandma Duff how dangerous it was. I tried a hundred times. But she would not listen. Up until today, I had thought Grandma Duff understood a little bit of Dog. She seemed to know when I wanted a snack. She seemed to understand when I asked for a head rub. She had no trouble when I told her I was in the habit of licking the plates before they were washed.

But when I barked at the snow fort, she did not understand a word I said. It was clear that she did not have a very large vocabulary in Dog.

At three o'clock I realized that the fort was way too high. I could not risk leaving it to

chase after the children. I knew I had to stay inside the walls—just in case. I sat down on the snow.

Actually, a rest was just what I needed.

Arnie and Beth and Jennie were piling the blocks. Katie had already left. She went to a movie with Pete. Mike and Grandma and Willie and John were still making blocks. The rest of the kids were trying to knock each other down with snowballs.

Fudge came and sat with me. He wanted to talk about reading lessons.

"I'll start after Grandma Duff goes home," I told Fudge.

"You mean Grandma Duff is going home?" said Fudge. He was shocked.

"She certainly is," I answered. "Day after tomorrow."

"Oh no," said Fudge. He was upset. "I like Grandma Duff."

"I like her, too," I said. "But she has too much energy. If she doesn't go home, I'll never make it."

"Make what?" asked Fudge.

I didn't bother to answer. That cat doesn't understand anything. He has more to learn than reading, I'm afraid.

I put my head on my paws. I pretended

48

to be asleep. That is the only way to keep Fudge from asking dumb questions. As soon as I close my eyes, Fudge goes away.

I lay there until Fudge left. Then I heard Grandma Duff say, "Let's all go inside and have hot chocolate!"

"What about the fort?" asked Arnie.

"We'll finish it later," said Grandma Duff.

I heard the sweet sound of boots crunching up the snow-covered porch steps. The door banged shut.

Finally. Peace and quiet. I sighed happily. Snow isn't such a bad place to snooze. Having a thick coat of fur beats a snowsuit any day. That's why it is better to be a dog. And if you are going to be a dog, it is always best to be a Saint Bernard.

CHAPTER EIGHT

AND THE WALLS CAME A-TUMBLING DOWN

I am only telling you this part of the story as it was told to me. I don't remember any of it. I also don't believe a word of it. Fudge told me this story. As you have already seen, Fudge is not very good at getting the facts right. But since I was not actually there, it is the best I can do.

Just remember one thing while you read this. A small, dumb cat told me the story.

Anyway, Arnie, Beth, Mike, Grandma Duff, and all the little maniacs went inside the house for hot chocolate. They made a big pot of it. Then they took some upstairs to Mr. and Mrs. Duff. They all sat around in the big bedroom. They talked and laughed and drank their hot chocolate. No one was thinking about me.

But soon it started to get dark. The children's parents came and picked them all up. They decided it was too late to work on the fort. Besides, the party was over. Then Katie and Pete came home from the movies. Grandma Duff decided it was time to make dinner.

They all went down to the kitchen. I was not there. But it was time for my dinner. So Arnie filled my bowl. He filled Fudge's bowl. Fudge ate up all his dinner. Still, I was not there. Then Fudge ate up half of my dinner. I was still not home yet.

After Fudge ate up half my dinner, they started to get worried. Where is Fred? Fred is always home by suppertime! Especially since Fudge arrived.

At first they thought I had been dog-napped. But who would dog-nap me? And how could they do it? I am far too tough for anyone to nap and live.

Then Arnie got very sad. He thought

maybe I was still mad about getting the tail pinned to my ear. That, of course, was after Katie suggested that perhaps I had finally gone crazy and run away from home. That is completely ridiculous. Dogs do not go crazy. Especially Saint Bernards with a lot of responsibility. But I can see why she would think that. Teenagers often go crazy.

Well, they all put their snowsuits, mittens, hats, scarves, and boots back on. They went looking for me.

The truth is that I was still in the snow fort. I was a wreck. I had been a wreck for days. I was more wrecked than I had ever been. I was so wrecked that I couldn't even eat any magazines. That's how bad it was.

Anyway, Grandma Duff was the one who finally found me. But that is not the humiliating part.

The humiliating part was that I had to be rescued. But it was not my fault. If anyone had listened to me, none of this would have happened.

What happened was that the snow fort fell

down. It was way too high—just as I had tried to tell them. But would they listen? Nope.

Anyway, the walls fell down and trapped me inside. Me—Fred the Fearless, The Great Houdini of Dogs, The Protector of the Careless!

I must say one thing. I didn't even try to get out. I didn't know the walls had fallen down. I didn't know I was trapped. I didn't even know I was being rescued. That is because I didn't *need* rescuing. Is this clear? It is clear to me.

Fudge said I slept through the whole thing.

That is not true. I wasn't asleep. They just *thought* I was asleep. I was daydreaming. I was thinking about that picture Mike had taken of me rescuing Katie from the cliff. I was dreaming about my picture on the front page of the newspaper. I was thinking about the speech I would make at the party held in my honor. I was trying to decide how big a medal I should get. I *certainly* was not sleeping. I just wasn't paying very close attention.

And even if I had been asleep, I would *not* have needed rescuing. Especially by a little old grandmother. I could have gotten out all by myself, thank you very much. I am not called the Great Houdini of Dogs for nothing.

But enough of all these lies. When I got inside, I was feeling a good deal better. Until I noticed that half of my dinner was gone.

Of course, I knew right away who had eaten it. I glowered at Fudge. He looked innocent.

"I deserved it," Fudge said.

"For what, may I ask?" I answered.

"I helped rescue you," said Fudge.

"First of all," I said, "I wasn't rescued."

"You were, too," said Fudge.

"And second of all," I said, "even if I *was* rescued, which I was not, you were not the one who did it. Grandma Duff did it."

"I showed her where to look," said Fudge.

I was about to tell Fudge what I thought about his story when Grandma Duff called my name. She put down a big bowl of hot milk for me.

I hate hot milk. But I drank it all up anyway. I did it to keep Fudge from getting any. It was the least I could do.

I went upstairs to lie down with Mr. and Mrs. Duff. I didn't want to be around anyone who was able to move.

Mr. Duff's nose looked like an apple. Mrs. Duff had pillows stuffed under her legs, her head, and her elbows. I had a bandage on my ear, and ice chunks between my toes. The room looked like a field hospital during World War II. That's also how it felt. Sometimes, life at the Duffs' can be rough.

CHAPTER NINE

AN HONORARY
SAINT BERNARD

Well, I slept very soundly that night. I was very, very tired!

The next day was better. For one thing, I got a good night's sleep. That helped. But was anyone else in that house tired? Nope. Katie, Arnie, and Grandma Duff were up at seven o'clock. But Grandma Duff was teaching the children how to knit. That meant they were staying inside—and out of trouble.

I decided I needed some time off.

Beth and Mike showed up. Mike showed everyone his latest photographs. He said he had taken the film to the One-Hour Photo place. One hour, my foot! If it only takes an hour, then how come it took a whole day?

Anyhow, the photo I was waiting for was in the group! What luck. It was the one of me rescuing Katie.

When no one was looking, I snatched the picture. I stuck it under the rug in the hall.

Beth and Mike stayed for knitting lessons. Beth has a new pet. Beth's new pet is a spider. She brought it over in a jar. I am not that fond of spiders. But as long as it stayed in the jar, I didn't mind. This spider was named Eleanor. Don't ask me why.

Grandma Duff asked Beth why she had named the spider Eleanor.

"She looks like an Eleanor," answered Beth.

I don't think that's a very good reason. But as I have said before, Beth can be strange. I like her anyway. Beth and I understand each other. She rescues animals. I rescue people. The only difference is that the people I rescue *need* rescuing. The animals she rescues do not always need rescuing. But why argue over a little thing like that?

Anyway, when they were all sitting on the couch knitting, I snuck out. I got the picture out from under the rug. I slipped out my dog door. I figured I had about two hours before they got bored with knitting and spiders and started getting into trouble.

I popped down to the office of the *Big Bluff News.* I slipped the photograph in through the mail slot on the door. Then I sat on the front step and barked and howled. Barking and howling always gets someone to the door. It was the only way to make sure the picture got into the right hands. Well, maybe not the *right* hands—but someone's hands at least.

After four minutes of barking and howling, one of the ladies came to the front door. Then another one came. Finally one of them bent down. I could see her showing the picture to the other one. They pointed at me. They smiled.

It was as good as done. Tomorrow I would

be front-page news. It was time to take a little walk and clear my head.

As I strolled down to the harbor, I passed a garbage heap. It was behind the grocery store. I thought maybe I would find a tasty bone in the trash. That's when I saw the very thing I needed! It was a small wooden barrel.

You see, I had been thinking . . .

Grandma Duff was really pretty okay. After all, she helped me take care of Mr. and Mrs. Duff. She ran up and down the stairs five thousand times carrying things. She helped me have a good birthday party for Arnie. She even helped me when I got stuck in the snow fort.

Not that I needed the help, of course. But Grandma Duff did not know that. She did the right thing.

I wanted to show her that I appreciated everything she did for my family. What better way could there be than to make her an honorary Saint Bernard?

This wooden barrel was perfect. It was just like the ones Saint Bernards carry around their necks. She could put it on a rope or something. She could wear it around her neck—just like a Saint Bernard!

I took it home. I hid it in the garage. I found a nice long piece of rope. It was only a little bit dirty.

The next morning, Grandma Duff was packing her things to leave. I went into the garage and got the gift. I took it up to her room. I put it right into her suitcase.

"Why, Fred," said Grandma Duff. "What have we here?"

She picked up the barrel. Then she smiled. She understood right away.

"Fred, this is the sweetest gift I have ever gotten," she said. "You are making me an honorary Saint Bernard! What a wonderful way to say thank you!"

She scratched my ear. I jumped up on the bed and pulled the rope out of the suitcase. I held it out to her.

"You mean I should *wear* the barrel?" she said with an odd look. "Like now?"

I barked. What else?

"Well, er," said Grandma Duff. She was at a loss for words. I could see that she was *very* grateful. She just didn't know how to tell me. I barked again. "It's rather heavy."

Heavy? Well, maybe. After all, Grandma Duff is little. She's old. She's weak. I really could not expect her to wear a heavy barrel around her neck. A big, strong Saint Bernard like me would have no trouble. Of course. I understood.

I barked and gave her a kiss on the cheek. Just then, Katie poked her head in the door.

"Are you ready, Grandma?" she asked.

"Indeed I am," said Grandma Duff. "Only this time, I want Fred to come to the station with us."

Grandma Duff smiled at me. Katie groaned.

"Oh, all right," Katie finally said. "At least, this time he's clean!"

See? I told you so. Whatever Grandma Duff wants, Grandma Duff gets. That's probably because she's so little and so weak.

I understand perfectly.

CHAPTER TEN

AN INDIAN WOULD BE BETTER

Well, I enjoyed the ride to the station. Usually I don't like to ride in the car. That is because the only time I go in the car is when I go to the vet.

I don't like the vet much. He talks in this dumb, cute way. I suppose he wants Mrs. Duff to think he is "good with animals." As far as I'm concerned, the only animal that man would be good with is a clam. But maybe that is an unkind thing to say about clams.

He says things like "This doesn't bother him" when he sticks a needle into me.

Needles hurt. What is he? Crazy?

He says things like "Dog food is a per-

65

fectly balanced food. You shouldn't give him leftovers." Dog food is not that great. You never see people eating it, do you? If leftovers are not good for me, how come they are good for people? And furthermore, if dog food is so good, why doesn't the vet eat it?

He says things like "It's not a good idea to let your dog go outside without a leash. He might get hit by a car."

People are the ones who need leashes. They are the ones who are always getting hit by cars. He gets everything backward.

I suppose the vet is nice. He just isn't too smart.

Anyway. I didn't mind this car trip at all. Mr. Duff drove. Arnie sat up front next to Mrs. Duff. That is because he's the smallest, and Mr. and Mrs. Duff are the biggest.

Katie and Grandma Duff and I, Fred, sat in the back. I sat next to the window. I stuck my head out. I like to do that. When we go fast, the wind blows my cheeks out. It makes this neat flapping noise.

We got to the station way ahead of time. We unloaded Grandma Duff's suitcases. I tried to keep everyone cornered over by the big clock on the station house. There was only one small mishap. Everybody made a big deal out of it. Personally, I didn't see what the fuss was all about.

When the bell started to clang, Arnie rushed over to the edge of the tracks. So I rushed over and grabbed the back of his jacket. I dragged him to the station house. The door was open. That was good. I decided Arnie was better off inside. So I dragged him into the station house. All the Duffs came in too. There were lots of people inside. I guess they thought it was warm in there or something. I thought it was hot as a steam bath.

The problem was Arnie's jacket. He wears this dark blue, slippery jacket stuffed with little fluffy feathers.

The jacket was very slippery. And I had to hold on to the jacket pretty hard. My tooth must have snagged something. Anyway, the jacket tore. All these little tiny fluffy feathers started puffing out of Arnie's jacket. For some reason, the whole station house filled with these feathers. It looked like it was snowing in there. Who would have guessed that one small jacket could have so many little fluffy feathers in it? Everyone had feathers stuck to them.

Mr. Duff called me a fathead. But I didn't mind. What's a few feathers when a child's safety is at stake?

Anyway, Grandma Duff got on the train. She had feathers in her hair and on her coat. She even had a feather on the corner of her lip. But *she* didn't mind. *She* was smiling.

"I had a lovely time at your birthday party, Arnie," she said when she kissed him good-bye.

I'm glad somebody did, I thought. I had a *terrible* time. But at least the party's over with—until next year, of course.

We all waved good-bye—from a safe distance. I made sure of that! Then we went

home. What a relief! I went right into the living room and lay down on the rug.

Of course, Fudge was waiting for me. No sooner had I settled down than Fudge curled up right next to me. I was too tired to tell him to get lost.

"Can you teach me how to read?" asked Fudge.

"Not now," I said.

"Tomorrow?" said Fudge.

"We'll see," I said.

"Good," said Fudge. "That means you'll teach me how to read tomorrow!"

I think that cat is deaf. He never hears anything right.

Just as I was falling asleep, Fudge gave me a poke.

"Now what?" I said.

"This is just like the Indians," said Fudge.

I opened one eye. "What Indians?"

"I saw a show on television," said Fudge. "It was about Indians."

"So what," I said.

"No," said Fudge. "What happened at the

birthday party was just like the Indians. You see, I saved your life."

"You did not," I said. I closed my eyes to make Fudge stop talking. But he wouldn't. He went right on yammering.

"With Indians, once you save someone's life," Fudge went on, "you are always responsible for them."

I was speechless.

"I promise I will always take care of you, Mom," he said. "Don't worry."

I groaned. Don't worry? Having Fudge take care of me was going to be a *big* worry. An Indian would be better.

I tried to fall asleep. But I couldn't.

What next?

(You should only know!)

THE END